Walt Disney's Sleeping Beauty

STORY ADAPTED BY
MONIQUE PETERSON

PICTURES BY **THE WALT DISNEY STUDIOS**
ADAPTED BY **NORM MCGARY**

A WELCOME BOOK

DISNEY
EDITIONS

New York

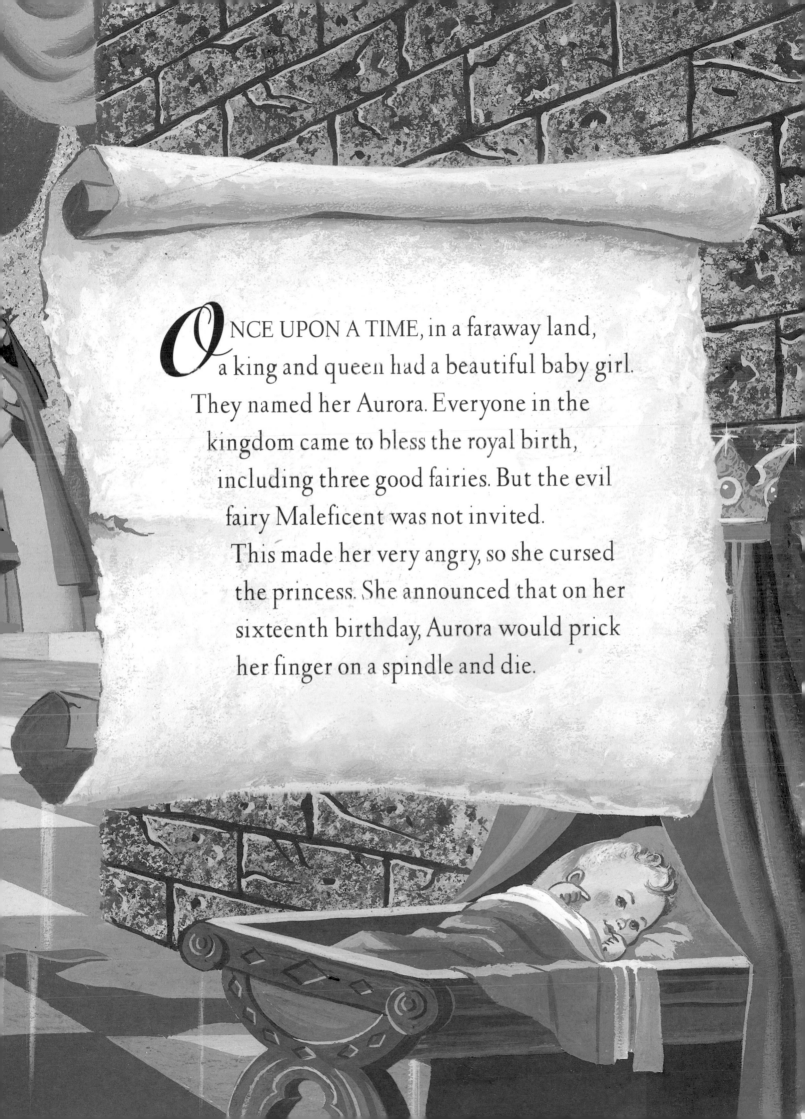

ONCE UPON A TIME, in a faraway land,
a king and queen had a beautiful baby girl.
They named her Aurora. Everyone in the
kingdom came to bless the royal birth,
including three good fairies. But the evil
fairy Maleficent was not invited.

This made her very angry, so she cursed
the princess. She announced that on her
sixteenth birthday, Aurora would prick
her finger on a spindle and die.

The king and queen were horrified. But the good fairies, Flora, Fauna, and Merryweather, came up with a plan to protect Princess Aurora from Maleficent.

They disguised themselves as peasants and
raised Aurora deep in the woods. To be extra safe,
the fairies agreed to stop using magic so that no
one—especially Maleficent—would suspect them.

Sixteen years went by, and no one discovered
Aurora's secret home. Her only companions were
the birds and fluffy-tailed squirrels and rabbits.

But the princess was never lonely, for she played
with her animal friends every day. She sang to them,
and told them about her dreams of falling in love.

On Princess Aurora's sixteenth birthday,
her dreams came true! Prince Phillip heard
a beautiful song in the forest and followed
the sound. He came upon Aurora singing,
and they fell in love at first sight. All Aurora's
forest friends shared in their joy as the
happy couple danced and danced.

Meanwhile, the fairies were planning a secret
birthday surprise. Fauna tried to whip up a fancy layer
cake. She simply opened a recipe book and started
mixing all the ingredients in a big bowl.

Flora wanted to make an extra-special dress. She used
Merryweather as a model. First, Flora cut a hole in the
center of the cloth for Aurora's feet to go through!

Poor Fauna didn't know the first thing about making a cake. She tried and tried and tried, but the only thing she could make was a gooey mess.

And Flora had never before made a dress. She snipped and clipped here and pinned and patched there, but she only succeeded in making Merryweather cry. Flora had stitched together a gown absolutely unfit for a princess.

Merryweather finally had enough of Flora and Fauna's nonsense. After sixteen years, it was time to get out their wands! They needed magic to clean up their mess! So, with a few simple whisks of their wands...

Fauna's cake rose to perfection with pink icing and brilliant candles. And Flora's fabric gathered itself, trimmed itself, and sewed itself together. In the blink of an eye, it became the finest gown a princess could dream to wear.

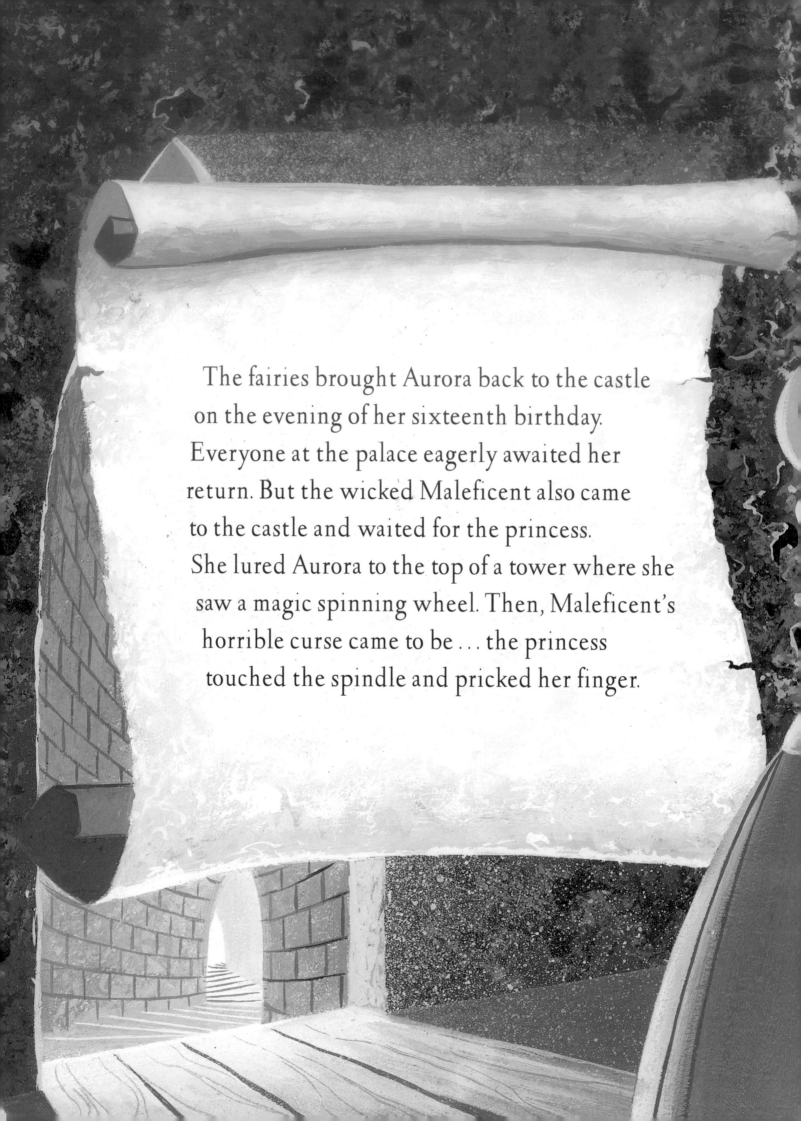

The fairies brought Aurora back to the castle
on the evening of her sixteenth birthday.
Everyone at the palace eagerly awaited her
return. But the wicked Maleficent also came
to the castle and waited for the princess.
She lured Aurora to the top of a tower where she
saw a magic spinning wheel. Then, Maleficent's
horrible curse came to be … the princess
touched the spindle and pricked her finger.

The princess fell to the floor. The fairies wept, for they couldn't stop Maleficent. But Aurora didn't die. The good fairies worked their magic so that the princess simply fell into a deep sleep. She would awaken only after the first kiss of her true love.

Flora, Fauna, and Merryweather couldn't bear to break the king's heart with the news of Aurora's fate. So they made everyone else in the castle sleep, too . . . all the guards, the ladies-in-waiting, even the king and queen.

Once the palace was totally quiet, the fairies
flew away with magical speed. They needed to find
the handsome prince who would break the spell.

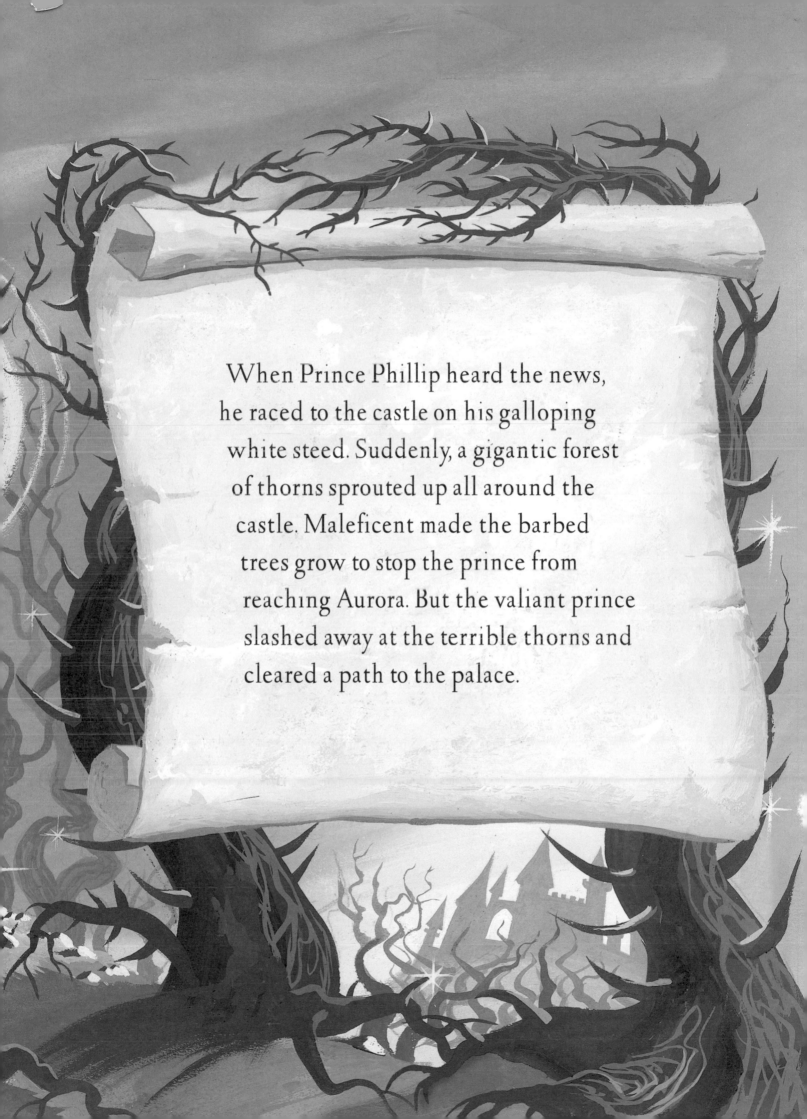

When Prince Phillip heard the news,
he raced to the castle on his galloping
white steed. Suddenly, a gigantic forest
of thorns sprouted up all around the
castle. Maleficent made the barbed
trees grow to stop the prince from
reaching Aurora. But the valiant prince
slashed away at the terrible thorns and
cleared a path to the palace.

As soon as the prince got to the palace, a fierce and furious dragon appeared before him. It was Maleficent, who used all her powers to transform herself into a fire-breathing dragon! The dragon blasted Phillip with a fiery blaze.

He stumbled back and nearly fell off the cliff. But the brave prince used his shield and hurled his mighty sword deep into the heart of the dragon. The monstrous Maleficent dropped dead, once and for all!

The prince dashed to Aurora's side and gave her the kiss of true love. The princess began to stir. She fluttered her eyelids open and awoke at last! Happiness filled her heart when she saw her handsome prince.

Then, the spell lifted. Yawning and stretching sounds could be heard throughout the entire castle. The king and queen and everyone else slowly woke from their slumber.

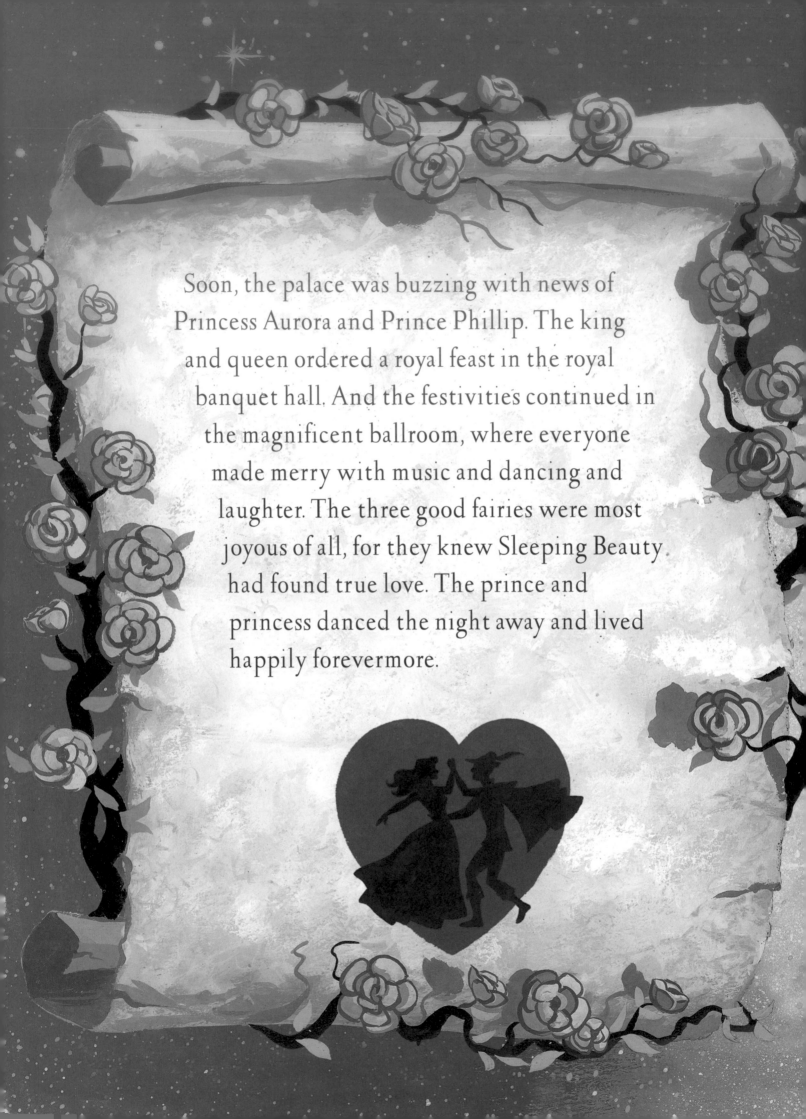

Soon, the palace was buzzing with news of
Princess Aurora and Prince Phillip. The king
and queen ordered a royal feast in the royal
banquet hall. And the festivities continued in
the magnificent ballroom, where everyone
made merry with music and dancing and
laughter. The three good fairies were most
joyous of all, for they knew Sleeping Beauty
had found true love. The prince and
princess danced the night away and lived
happily forevermore.